Romulus and Remus

by Mick Gowar and Andrew Breakspeare

W
FRANKLIN WATTS
LONDON·SYDNEY

Numitor, king of Alba Longa,
was very happy. His daughter
had given birth to twin boys.

The princes were named Romulus and Remus. King Numitor gave each grandson a gold necklace.

"They will be kings of Alba Longa one day," said Numitor proudly.

But Numitor's brother, Amulius,
was jealous. He wanted to be king
of Alba Longa. He gathered some
soldiers and raced to the palace.

"I'm the king now!" he told his
brother, Numitor. "Leave at once!"
He sent a soldier to get the princes,
Romulus and Remus.

Wicked Amulius took the basket with Romulus and Remus inside and pushed it into the river.

The little basket sped down
the river until it hit a bank.
The twins fell out with a bump.

A she-wolf found the twins by the
river. She carried them back to
her den under a fig tree, where
a woodpecker lived.

The wolf and the woodpecker fed
the twins with milk and figs.

Romulus and Remus did not like to share. They fought every day. "The figs are mine!" cried Romulus. "No, they're mine!" cried Remus.

One day, a shepherd heard the
twins fighting. He chased away
the wolf and the woodpecker.

"I'll take you home," he told the twins. He looked after them as if they were his own sons.

When they were older, Romulus and Remus went back to Alba Longa. Everyone knew who they were by their gold necklaces.

"Welcome princes of Alba Longa,"
said the old king's minister.
"Your grandfather, Numitor,
needs your help!"

Romulus and Remus raced to the
palace with Numitor. Amulius was
shocked. He thought the twins
had drowned.

"You're not the true king of Alba Longa!" said Romulus and Remus. There was a fight and Amulius was killed.

Numitor was king once again.
All the people cheered and
brought him wonderful gifts.

But the twins started to fight.

"I want to be king," cried Romulus.

"So do I," screamed Remus.

"Why don't you build you own city?" said Numitor. "Then you can *both* be kings."

"I'll be king first," said Romulus.

"No, *I* will," said Remus.

"We'll build our city here!"
said Romulus.

"No, *here!*" said Remus.

They had a terrible fight.
Romulus picked up a rock and
threw it at Remus, killing him.

"I'm the only king!" said Romulus.
"Everyone must help me to build
a wonderful city.

I will call it Rome, after my own
name. One day it will be the
greatest city in the whole world."

But the wolf and the shepherd were sad. Every time they saw Romulus's wonderful new city, they thought of poor Remus.

Hopscotch has been specially designed to fit the requirements of the Literacy Framework. It offers real books by top authors and illustrators for children developing their reading skills. There are 63 Hopscotch stories to choose from:

Marvin, the Blue Pig
ISBN 978 0 7496 4619 6

Plip and Plop
ISBN 978 0 7496 4620 2

The Queen's Dragon
ISBN 978 0 7496 4618 9

Flora McQuack
ISBN 978 0 7496 4621 9

Willie the Whale
ISBN 978 0 7496 4623 3

Naughty Nancy
ISBN 978 0 7496 4622 6

Run!
ISBN 978 0 7496 4705 6

The Playground Snake
ISBN 978 0 7496 4706 3

"Sausages!"
ISBN 978 0 7496 4707 0

Bear in Town
ISBN 978 0 7496 5875 5

Pippin's Big Jump
ISBN 978 0 7496 4710 0

Whose Birthday Is It?
ISBN 978 0 7496 4709 4

The Princess and the Frog
ISBN 978 0 7496 5129 9

Flynn Flies High
ISBN 978 0 7496 5130 5

Clever Cat
ISBN 978 0 7496 5131 2

Moo!
ISBN 978 0 7496 5332 3

Izzie's Idea
ISBN 978 0 7496 5334 7

Roly-poly Rice Ball
ISBN 978 0 7496 5333 0

I Can't Stand It!
ISBN 978 0 7496 5765 9

Cockerel's Big Egg
ISBN 978 0 7496 5767 3

How to Teach a Dragon Manners
ISBN 978 0 7496 5873 1

The Truth about those Billy Goats
ISBN 978 0 7496 5766 6

Marlowe's Mum and the Tree House
ISBN 978 0 7496 5874 8

The Truth about Hansel and Gretel
ISBN 978 0 7496 4708 7

The Best Den Ever
ISBN 978 0 7496 5876 2

ADVENTURES

Aladdin and the Lamp
ISBN 978 0 7496 6692 7

Blackbeard the Pirate
ISBN 978 0 7496 6690 3

George and the Dragon
ISBN 978 0 7496 6691 0

Jack the Giant-Killer
ISBN 978 0 7496 6693 4

TALES OF KING ARTHUR

1. The Sword in the Stone
ISBN 978 0 7496 6694 1

2. Arthur the King
ISBN 978 0 7496 6695 8

3. The Round Table
ISBN 978 0 7496 6697 2

4. Sir Lancelot and the Ice Castle
ISBN 978 0 7496 6698 9

TALES OF ROBIN HOOD

Robin and the Knight
ISBN 978 0 7496 6699 6

Robin and the Monk
ISBN 978 0 7496 6700 9

Robin and the Silver Arrow
ISBN 978 0 7496 6703 0

Robin and the Friar
ISBN 978 0 7496 6702 3

FAIRY TALES

The Emperor's New Clothes
ISBN 978 0 7496 7421 2

Cinderella
ISBN 978 0 7496 7417 5

Snow White
ISBN 978 0 7496 7418 2

Jack and the Beanstalk
ISBN 978 0 7496 7422 9

The Three Billy Goats Gruff
ISBN 978 0 7496 7420 5

The Pied Piper of Hamelin
ISBN 978 0 7496 7419 9

Goldilocks and the Three Bears
ISBN 978 0 7496 7903 3

Hansel and Gretel
ISBN 978 0 7496 7904 0

The Three Little Pigs
ISBN 978 0 7496 7905 7

Rapunzel
ISBN 978 0 7496 7906 4

Little Red Riding Hood
ISBN 978 0 7496 7907 1

Rumpelstiltskin
ISBN 978 0 7496 7908 8

HISTORIES

Toby and the Great Fire of London
ISBN 978 0 7496 7410 6

Pocahontas the Peacemaker
ISBN 978 0 7496 7411 3

Grandma's Seaside Bloomers
ISBN 978 0 7496 7412 0

Hoorah for Mary Seacole
ISBN 978 0 7496 7413 7

Remember the 5th of November
ISBN 978 0 7496 7414 4

Tutankhamun and the Golden Chariot
ISBN 978 0 7496 7415 1

MYTHS

Icarus, the Boy Who Flew
ISBN 978 0 7496 7992 7 *
ISBN 978 0 7496 8000 8

Perseus and the Snake Monster
ISBN 978 0 7496 7993 4 *
ISBN 978 0 7496 8001 5

Odysseus and the Wooden Horse
ISBN 978 0 7496 7994 1 *
ISBN 978 0 7496 8002 2

Persephone and the Pomegranate Seeds
ISBN 978 0 7496 7995 8 *
ISBN 978 0 7496 8003 9

Romulus and Remus
ISBN 978 0 7496 7996 5 *
ISBN 978 0 7496 8004 6

Thor's Hammer
ISBN 978 0 7496 7997 2*
ISBN 978 0 7496 8005 3

No Dinner for Anansi
ISBN 978 0 7496 7998 9 *
ISBN 978 0 7496 8006 0

Gelert the Brave
ISBN 978 0 7496 7999 6*
ISBN 978 0 7496 8007 7

* hardback